the Golden Cockerel

From the Original Russian Fairy Tale
of Alexander Pushkin

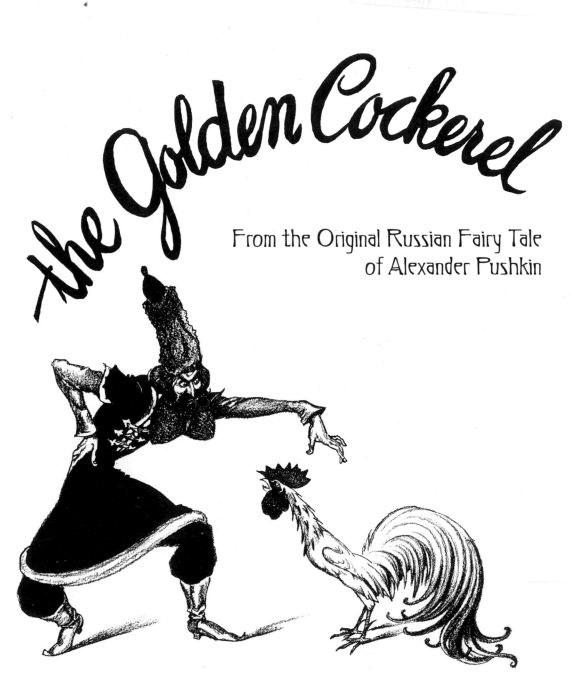

WILLY POGÁNY

the Golden Cockerel

From the Original Russian Fairy Tale
of Alexander Pushkin

Retold by
Elaine Pogány
and Illustrated by
Willy Pogány

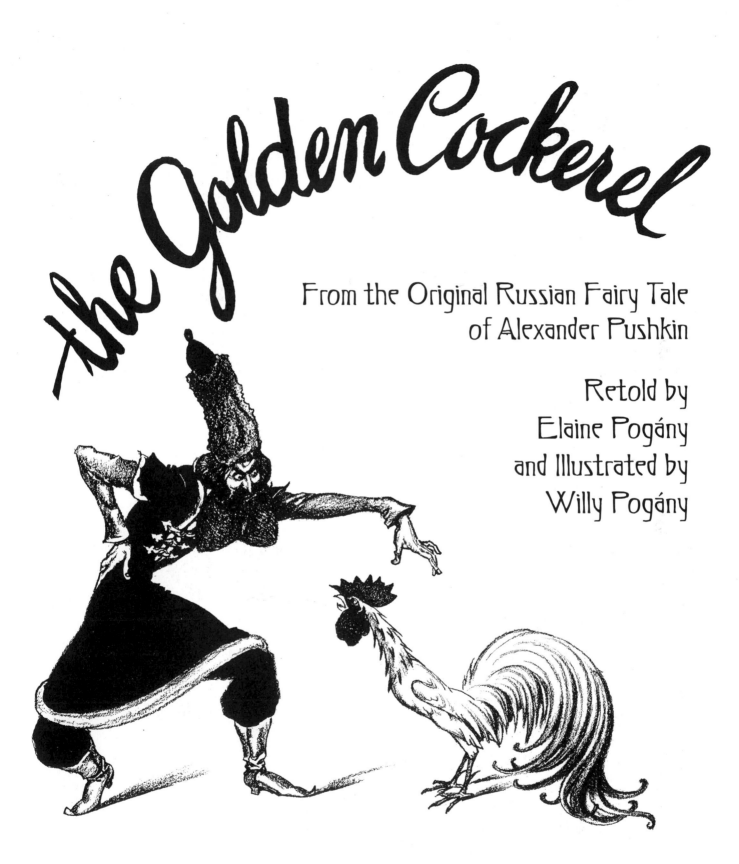

DOVER PUBLICATIONS, INC.
Mineola, New York

Bibliographical Note

The Golden Cockerel: From the Original Russian Fairy Tale of Alexander Pushkin, first published by Dover Publications, Inc., in 2013, is an unabridged republication of the work originally published by Thomas Nelson and Sons, New York, in 1938.

International Standard Book Number
ISBN-13: 978-0-486-49115-8
ISBN-10: 0-486-49115-3

Manufactured in the United States by Courier Corporation
49115301   2013
www.doverpublications.com

ONCE upon a time in a far away country there lived an old King named Dadon. He had been a mighty warrior in his younger days, but now he was very fat and very lazy. He liked to spend his time feasting and taking long naps on his huge feather bed. He loved his feather bed.

Willy Pogány

Very often he wandered down to the enormous palace kitchens. He enjoyed watching the cooks prepare delicious foods for his festive board. And what a busy kitchen it was! There were great processions of maids and knaves carrying pies and roasts. Jolly fat cooks stirred mixtures in huge bowls, while ducks and pigs were turning on the spit. Out of the great big ovens there came delicious cakes all decorated with sugar roses and other wonderful goodies.

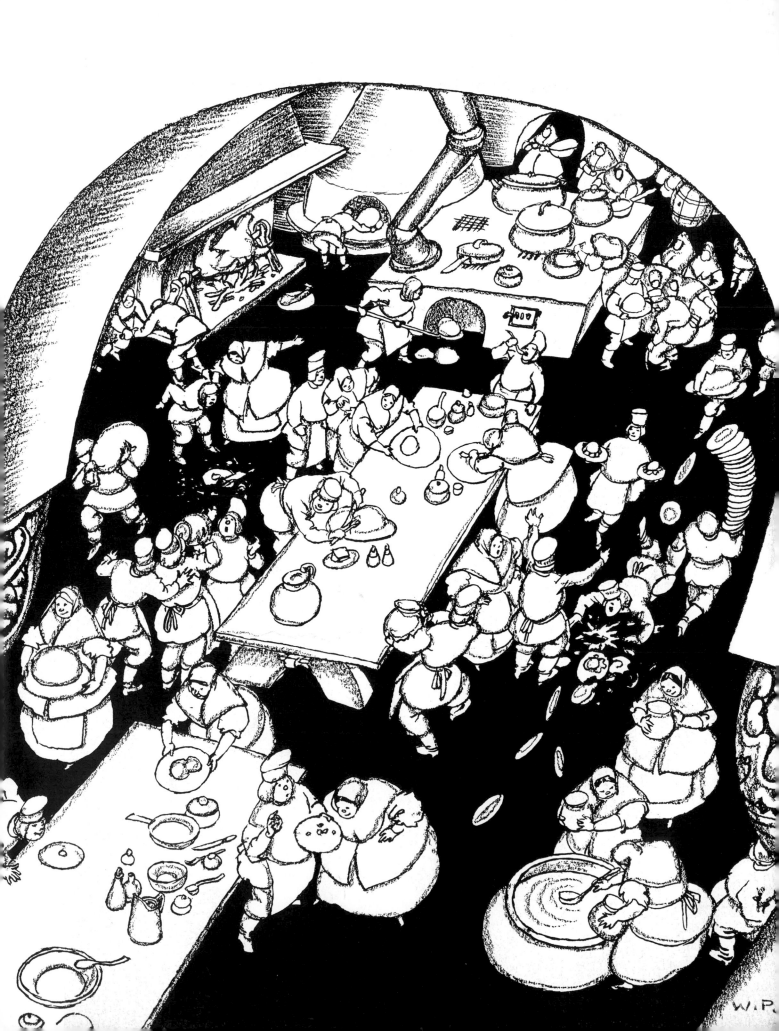

If it had not been for the evil ruler of the Dark Mountains, which lay beyond his Kingdom, old Dadon would have been very happy.

This ruler was really a wicked Magician who could not bear to see anyone happy.

He lived in a dark, cold cave, and night after night, by the light of a million fireflies, he studied old books. He was always hoping to find more and more ways of making people unhappy.

The old King's jolly, care-free life made him very angry. So the wicked Magician gathered his armies together from all the darkest corners of the Dark Mountains and sent them forth to attack the peaceful realm of King Dadon.

And then the poor old King had a dreadful time! No sooner did he send an army to the North, than the Magician's armies would attack from the South. And when Dadon sent his warriors to the East, the enemy would surely come from the West. So the King's armies never got a chance to fight the mysterious foe.

All these troubles kept the King from taking his nice long naps in the huge feather bed, and he didn't like this at all! So he called a meeting of his wise men, the boyars. He was sure they could tell him from which direction the enemy would come.

The boyars sat before the King and thought day and night over this mighty problem. After many days and many nights, they finally decided that the only one who could help the King was the fortune teller. So old Dadon commanded that the fortune teller come quickly. But the boyars shook their heads at this order, and then the eldest and wisest arose with great dignity. He stroked his long, grey beard and said, "But, mighty Dadon, the fortune teller has been dead for many, many years."

This bad news made the King very unhappy. Then all the wise men began to talk at once.

"If our fortune teller were alive," said one of them, "he could save our kingdom with his magic mixture of beans, cooked in a large iron pot with a strange and secret herb."

"Beans!" said another boyar. "Pooh! Who ever heard such nonsense! Now I heard of a witch who could foretell the future with grains of sand."

"Sand!" screeched another boyar. "How silly! By the stars alone can one tell the future."

Soon the royal halls fairly shook with "Beans" – "Sand" – "Piffle" – "Stars" – "Nonsense!" as each boyar shouted as loudly as he could.

The King by this time was almost weeping with rage and disappointment. "Enough!" he shouted, pounding his sceptre on the floor, "Away with all of you! You have brought me no help in my hour of need."

The boyars had never before seen jolly old Dadon in such a temper. They looked at each other in surprise. They were deeply hurt at his ungratefulness. Were they not the wisest men in the kingdom? And had they not thought and thought for days and days to help him?

Just when all seemed black with despair, there suddenly appeared an old, old man, carrying a bundle under his arm. He approached the throne, bowed deeply before the King and said, "Hail, O mighty King! I knew well your great-great-grandfather, and his grandfather before him. Tales of your great distress have reached my ears and I have brought you a gift."

He reached in the bundle and brought forth a Golden Cockerel. "Take this bird, O Majesty!" he said, "Place him on a spire atop one of the turrets of your castle. He will watch over your kingdom. If all is well, he will sit peaceful and quiet. But if there be a sign of danger, of enemies advancing to

destroy and pillage your lands, then this Golden Cockerel will begin to crow:

> *Cock-a-doodle-do!*
> *Awake! Arise! The foe's at hand!*
> *Seize your arms! Defend your land!*
> *Cock-a-doodle-do!*

and he will flap his wings and turn to whence the danger is coming."

Now the King listened hopefully to the old man's story, without really believing a word of it. And all the wise men looked down their noses. But poor tired Dadon was willing to try anything.

He commanded that the bird be placed on the spire. To his great delight he found that the old man had spoken the truth, for the Golden Cockerel flapped his wings and crowed:

> *Cock-a-doodle-do!*
> *All is peaceful,*
> *All is well.*
> *Cock-a-doodle-do!*

The old King fairly bounced with happiness and glee. He even forgot that he was angry with the boyars.

"How can I ever thank you?" the King asked the old, old man. "Surely there is some wish of yours that I might grant. Name anything you choose and it shall be yours."

The old man bowed politely and said, "I will remember your promise." Then he left, and no sooner was he outside the palace gate than he began to cackle with laughter. "Ho! Ho! Ho!" he laughed, until he could hardly stop, for he was none other than the evil Magician of the Dark Mountains, disguised as a kindly old man. He was very, very pleased because at last he had found a way to trick the King.

Peacefully two years went by and the Golden Cockerel sat quietly on his spire. The old King spent his days feasting on rich and delicious foods and taking long naps on his huge feather bed.

And then there was great excitement in the kingdom, for the King's only son, the brave Prince Igor, had fallen in love with the beautiful Princess Tatiana. Splendid preparations were being made for their wedding and the people went about singing and laughing.

One afternoon, the King was taking his usual nap in his big feather bed. His court ladies, who had gathered around the bed to drive the flies away with their silken handkerchiefs, slowly, one by one, dropped off to sleep. Even the faithful housekeeper, Dunya, was at last overcome by drowsiness and put her red head down on the edge of the bed. The only sound to be heard was the loud snoring of the old King. His crown was tipped over his nose and on his face was a happy smile. He was dreaming a magnificent dream of mince pies and strawberry tarts and other good things to eat.

Suddenly, outside, the Golden Cockerel began to stir. Then, arching his neck and wildly flapping his wings, he crowed a mighty warning:

Cock-a-doodle-do!
Awake! Arise! The foe's at hand!
Seize your arms! Defend your land!
Cock-a-doodle-do!

and he pointed in the direction of the East.

The Golden Cockerel's warning was heard from one end of the land to the other. The people rushed here and there in fright, for they knew that great danger was upon them.

Inside the palace everyone seemed to be running up and down the stairs. The Generals were running about looking for their swords and helmets. The soldiers were looking for the Generals, and the court ladies were very busy packing baskets of good things to eat for their favorite warriors.

General Pushka rushed into the palace and found the old King still asleep. "Awake!" he shouted, shaking him. "Awake! Great danger threatens!!"

The King opened his eyes and yawned. "Who is it? What is it? Where?" he asked, still half asleep.

"The Golden Cockerel has warned us. You
see, he is pointing to the East," explained the ex-
cited General. And at this moment the Cockerel
crowed again, even more mightily than before:

Cock-a-doodle-do!
Awake! Arise! The foe's at hand!
Seize your arms! Defend your land!
Cock-a-doodle-do!

"The horrid thing," said the King, shaking
his sleepy head. "Just as I was having the loveliest
dream, too. However," he said with a deep sigh, "I
suppose I must look after the affairs of State."

WILLY POGÁNY

The King got out of his feather bed and climbed up on his throne. He then sent for Prince Igor. "My son," he said, kissing him on each cheek, "you shall lead my armies against the foe. I am getting a bit too old to attend to these things."

The Prince bade his father farewell and then took leave of the beautiful Tatiana. The poor Princess, with tears in her eyes, begged the Prince to take great care of himself.

With waving banners the soldiers marched away and the old King went back to his feather bed and to his gentle slumbers and sweet dreams.

A year and a day went by with not a word of news from Prince Igor and his army. The poor Princess Tatiana wept night and day. "Something terrible has befallen my beloved Prince," she cried.

One day King Dadon was so worried that he
could not even eat his dinner. Dunya, the faithful
housekeeper, was trying to tempt him with dainty
tidbits. The court musicians struck up a gay tune,
and the court dancers and jesters tried their best to
make him smile. But the poor King only felt sadder and sadder. With a deep, deep sigh, he left the
table and retired to the sweet forgetfulness of his
big feather bed.

Just as the King had fallen off to sleep the
Golden Cockerel crowed again, and this time so
mightily that the whole palace trembled:

Cock-a-doodle-do!
Awake! Arise! The foe's at hand!
Seize your arms! Defend your land!
Cock-a-doodle-do!

and again he pointed to the East.

General Pushka rushed in to wake the King
and shouted, "O mighty King, new danger threatens! Awake! Awake!"

The King was very much vexed. "That bird!"
he mumbled, "always waking me at the wrong
time! Call out my armies!!" he shouted to the General. "This time I shall lead them against the foe."

25

It was hard work squeezing the very fat King into his old suit of armor. But with the help of most of the courtiers and the royal blacksmith, Dadon was finally ready. All the people cheered as he rode off to battle at the head of his armies.

Late one night, after many weary days of marching, the King and his army came to a deep, dark valley in the mountains. On the branches of bare trees giant crows sat motionless, their round, fiery eyes gleaming in the blackness of the night.

When the moon sent its first rays over this gloomy place, the King beheld Prince Igor and all his warriors standing straight and stiff in the moonlight. To his amazement, he discovered that they had all been turned into stone! And Dadon

knew that the wicked Magician had used his evil powers again. Great tears rolled down the poor old King's fat cheeks and into his big beard.

Just at this moment, in the center of the valley, a huge and beautiful tent slowly rose from the ground. In the bright moonlight the tent could be seen slowly opening. Out of it marched a gorgeous parade of damsels and courtiers, musicians and guards. Then came a most beautiful lady, the Princess Shamaka, Daughter of the Moon. Dadon stood bewitched by her beauty. He forgot all his sadness as she came toward him smiling. Her voice made the old King think of tinkling bells as she said, "Welcome, O most powerful and wondrous King! Welcome to my land of enchantment."

"Will you marry me, O beautiful Princess?" begged the King.

"It would be a great honor to be your Queen, O mighty King," answered the Princess, with a deep curtsy. "Yes, I will marry you."

So King Dadon and the Princess Shamaka drove away to his palace in a carriage drawn by two snow white horses. The King's armies followed the carriage, the stone Prince Igor and his stone soldiers marching stiffly at the rear.

The great procession that marched back into the city was a wonderful sight. At the head of it came the enchanted subjects of the Princess of the Moon. There were giants, dwarfs, one-eyed men, men with two left legs and two left hands, big-headed men and small-headed men, men with birds' heads, men with the heads of giraffes, and other strange and wondrous looking people, all dressed in brilliant robes studded with diamonds, rubies, emeralds, sapphires, and other precious stones and embroidered with gold.

Then came the carriage with King Dadon and the beautiful Princess Shamaka. All the people cheered and waved their colored handkerchiefs, and the King stood up and bowed deeply to his loyal subjects.

Suddenly, out of nowhere, the wicked Magician appeared, again dressed as an old man. He wended his way through the crowd to the royal carriage. And looking at the beautiful Princess Shamaka, he said, "Great King, it is I, and I have come to get my reward for giving you the Golden Cockerel who brought you this good fortune."

"Welcome," answered the King. "Tell me of your wish and it shall be granted."

"King Dadon," the Magician went on, "I ask as my reward the beautiful Princess of the Moon."

"You must have lost your senses," shouted the King. He was terribly angry at this outrageous request. "Come! Come!" he said, "ask something reasonable and it shall be yours. But the Princess, never!"

"You promised," snarled the Magician. Then he laughed a very wicked laugh. "Do you know who I am? I will show you!" And with this, the old, old man vanished quick as a wink, and there stood the evil Magician of the Dark Mountains.

WILLY POGÁNY

"I'll teach you to break your promise!" he shrieked. "All my life I have wanted the Princess of the Moon. It was I who turned the man she loved into that Golden Cockerel. It was I who lured you to her country and bewitched her so that she was willing to come with you. For only if she is brought to me by a mortal can I have her." Once more he laughed his wicked laugh. He was very happy for he saw that everyone about him was feeling quite miserable.

And then, just as the evil Magician reached out to claim the Princess Shamaka, lo and behold! from the top of the spire the Golden Cockerel let out a mighty crow. Too late the Magician saw the bird swooping down at him. Before he could move to save himself, the Golden Cockerel had pecked him hard on the head. And the wicked ruler of the Dark Mountains dropped dead.

Then the Golden Cockerel flew over to the sad and beautiful Princess Tatiana and said, "Do not be so sad, O Princess! Now that this evil creature is no more I can help you. Pluck the golden

feather under my left wing, and with it touch your
Prince Igor and all his soldiers."

The Princess did as she was bidden, and fairly
danced with joy as the stone Prince and his army
all came to life. She then touched all those who had
been bewitched, including the subjects of the Princess of the Moon. They all resumed their natural
shapes and forgot everything that had happened
to them before.

The old King, having been touched with the
feather, was no longer in love with the beautiful

Princess Shamaka. He still noticed, though, that she was very pretty.

Princess Tatiana, the golden feather still in her hand, thanked the Golden Cockerel for all the good he had done. She brushed him, too, with the golden feather, and he turned into a handsome Prince. With a joyous shout, he embraced the Princess Shamaka, and she was so happy to see her dear Prince again that she cried with joy.

At last, after days of feasting and rejoicing, Princess Shamaka and her Prince said good-by to the King and his subjects and rode off in their carriage drawn by the snow white horses.

The next day Prince Igor and Princess Tatiana were married amid great splendor. The wedding feast was the richest ever seen, and old King Dadon ate three times more than enough, and fell fast asleep at the table. The faithful Dunya called for the King's feather bed, and they laid him gently upon it without disturbing his sweet slumber.

The musicians changed their gay and lively tune to a soft lullaby, and the Prince and the Princess, and all the wedding guests joined in, singing and humming softly.